Ladybird books are widely available, but in case of
difficulty may be ordered by post or telephone from:

Ladybird Books – Cash Sales Department
Littlegate Road Paignton Devon TQ3 3BE
Telephone 0803 554761

A catalogue record for this book is available
from the British Library

Published by Ladybird Books Ltd Loughborough Leicestershire UK
LADYBIRD and the device of a Ladybird are trademarks of Ladybird Books Ltd

DISNEP

THE · LITTLE
MERMAID

Stormy the Wild Seahorse

Ladybird

Ariel a mermaid princess was in a mischievous mood. She had spent the morning teasing her older sisters in the palace, and had now decided it was time for a swim.

Playfully scooping up her friend Flounder and Sebastian her music teacher, Ariel swirled and dived through the water until she came to the royal stables.

Sebastian tried to protest, but it was no use.

Ariel stopped suddenly when she came to a cave. "Look! A giant seahorse!" she gasped in delight.

The seahorse neighed and snorted pitifully, trying to back away, as the little mermaid approached.

"Easy boy, easy," she said. "I won't hurt you. Poor thing! It's terrible to keep a wild creature tied up like this."

An old merman appeared at her side. "Keep your distance, Princess," he warned. "Stormy is too wild to tame and too bad tempered to love!"

But Ariel refused to believe him. "Some day," she thought to herself, "I'm going to ride that wild seahorse!"

Leaving the stables behind, Ariel swam away with her friends.

"Oh, it's going to be wonderful, Flounder!" she cried, explaining her plan. "All we have to do is convince Daddy to let me ride Stormy. I will ask at dinner tonight."

"Stormy?" laughed King Triton and Ariel's sisters that evening. "That wild seahorse would throw you off in an instant."

"But he let me swim right up and pet him," cried Ariel, looking defiantly at her father.

"You – *petted* him!" thundered her father, realising that his youngest daughter was not joking. "Ariel, I forbid you to go near that seahorse. He's much too dangerous."

Ariel swam to her room, sobbing.

"Cheer up," said Flounder. "There's lots of other things we can do than ride a giant seahorse."

"But why won't Daddy let me do what I want?" asked the angry Princess. "He's so mean!"

"I know what Ariel's thinking," said the King regretfully, when his other daughters had left the dining room. "She thinks I'm mean!"

"Your Majesty? Mean?" repeated Sebastian in surprise. "Ridiculous!"

"But I must make sure she does not disobey me," continued King Triton. "Sebastian, I want you to guard that seahorse stallion. I'm counting on you."

The crab scuttled away at the first opportunity. But in the hallway he met Ariel.

"Sebastian!" she whispered. "I'm going to see Stormy tonight, and you're going to be my look-out. I'm counting on you."

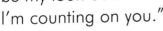

The music teacher curled up in his shell in despair. "*He* has me looking out for *her*! *She* has me looking out for *him*! But who's going to look out for *ME*?" he muttered.

At midnight Sebastian stood guard at the royal stables. His foot slipped on a clam near the entrance to Stormy's cave.

"Ouch!" said the shellfish. "Be careful, we sleep here."

Stormy whinnied loudly, scenting strangers nearby. Ariel and Flounder had also arrived.

"Sssh!" whispered the Princess to the frightened seahorse. "There's nothing to fear. One day, you and…"

"Ariel!" stormed the King behind her. "You disobeyed me. For your own good, I'm selling Stormy to a seahorse trader. You leave me no choice."

"You don't care what's best for me," cried Ariel, swimming out of the cave. "You want to tie me down, just like Stormy!"

Ariel went to her room, but she was determined to return to the cave before daybreak. She waited until she was certain her father was asleep and then crept quietly out of the palace.

She untied Stormy and leapt onto his back. "We'll ride to the edge of the sea," she sang. "Let's go!"

Sebastian watched secretly in the shadows. "Oh, dear! This means trouble!" he gulped. "I'd better send a message to the King."

King Triton came at once. "I knew this would happen," he cried.

"Don't worry! I've saddled the horses," said the old merman. "We'll get her back! If I know Stormy, he'll take her right into the Wilderness."

"We'll leave at once!" ordered the King.

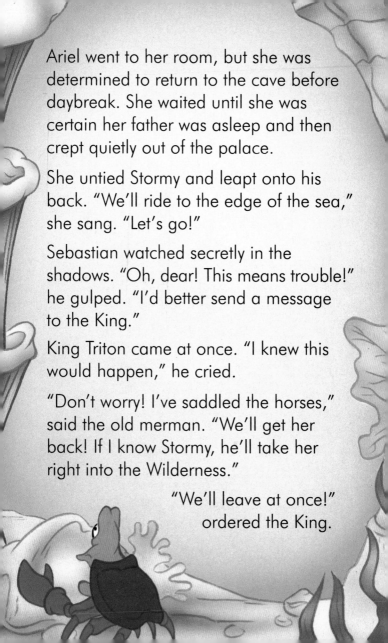

"Come on, Sebastian!" said Flounder, grabbing the reins of another seahorse. "We've got to save Ariel! *Away!*"

"I'm coming," groaned Sebastian and he gripped onto the seahorse's tail.

Far away, Ariel held on tightly to Stormy's mane as he sped through the shadowy ocean.

"Oh, no! The Wilderness!" she cried, realising where they were heading. "Stop! Stop, Stormy! Noooo!"

The giant seahorse whinnied victoriously and raced along even faster.

Close to the Wilderness, two seahorse rustlers were setting up camp for the night. "Do you think we'll catch any giant seahorses tomorrow?" asked the younger one.

"I don't know, kid," muttered the other. "I should think we'll be lucky to catch a glimpse of one!"

The two rustlers looked up in surprise as Stormy raced above them. They could not believe their eyes.

"Stormy! Slow down!" panicked Ariel. "You're going too fast!" She pulled with all her might on the seahorse's reins.

At last Stormy obeyed and slowed down. He whinnied, exhausted.

"Phew!" gasped Ariel. "That was *some* ride. We'd better rest for a while before we go home."

She pulled Stormy up to a stop, and they went to sleep on a rock.

Meanwhile the search for the little mermaid continued.

"Ariel! Ariel! Where are you?" shouted King Triton, his words echoing eerily round the rugged wasteland of the Wilderness.

"Where are you?" repeated Flounder and Sebastian.

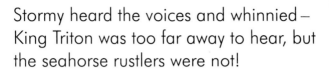

Stormy heard the voices and whinnied—
King Triton was too far away to hear, but
the seahorse rustlers were not!

As they charged forwards, tossing their
lassos, Stormy reared up and tried
desperately to escape. But it was no use.
The rustlers caught him and made their
way back to their camp.

Ariel woke to Stormy's pitiful cries. She followed the sound until she came to the rustlers' hiding place.

As the two horse thieves slept, Ariel gently untied Stormy, climbed on his back and sped away. Stormy neighed loudly in delight.

Roused from their sleep, the rustlers raced to their own horses and gave chase.

Ariel desperately tried to find a way out of the Wilderness, heading down a deep gorge. A ledge of rock jutted out in front of her, but it was too late to stop. The little mermaid Princess struck her head and toppled from Stormy's back. She plunged unconscious to the bottom of the ravine.

Stormy turned and hurtled after her. He swooped down and caught her on his back. Filled with fury he charged at the rustlers and sent them flying.

Stormy could hear familiar voices in the distance and made his way to the search party – with Ariel still slumped over his back.

"Ariel!" cried King Triton in dismay. "We must get you back to the palace!"

The palace doctor was called for at once. "She's going to be all right," he said. "You can talk to her for a while."

"Ariel," said her father gently, "can you hear me, my dear?"

"Where's Stormy?" she asked, slowly opening her eyes.

"That... That magnificent seahorse is too wild for you," said Triton, thinking he would need to go through the argument again.

"You're right," agreed Ariel, looking into her father's surprised eyes. "I understand now!"

Two days later Ariel returned with her father to the royal stables to release Stormy.

"He'll never be happy here," said the King. "You were right, it's better that he is free to roam where he wishes."

"Goodbye, Stormy," shouted Ariel, as the seahorse raced away. "I'll never forget you!"

And Stormy whinnied happily in reply.

"I'm proud of you, Ariel," said her father, leading her into another cave. "I know he's not Stormy… but here is Seabiscuit. He's much more your kind of seahorse!"

"Oh, I quite agree," she said, taking the reins from the merman. "Race you home, Daddy," she cried.

And with a happy laugh, Ariel and her father returned to the palace.